This book belongs to

AN AUSSIE NIGHT BEFORE CHRISTMAS

For Varieta - a giver all year round.

KN

Scholastic Press
345 Pacific Highway
Lindfield NSW 2070
An imprint of Scholastic Australia Pty Limited (ABN 11 000 614 577)
PO Box 579
Gosford NSW 2250
www.scholastic.com.au

Part of the Scholastic Group
Sydney • Auckland • New York • Toronto • London • Mexico City
• New Delhi • Hong Kong • Buenos Aires • Puerto Rico

First published by Scholastic Australia in 2005.
Reprinted 2005, 2006 and 2007.
Text copyright © Yvonne Morrison, 2005.
Illustrations copyright © Kilmeny Niland, 2005.

National Library of Australia Cataloguing-in-Publication entry
Morrison, Yvonne, 1972- .
    Aussie night before Christmas.
    For children aged 4+.
    ISBN 978 1 86504 653 2.
    1. Santa Claus - Juvenile poetry. 2. Christmas - Juvenile
    poetry. I. Niland, Kilmeny. II. Morre, Clement Clarke,
    1779-1863. Night before Christmas. III. Title.
NZ821.3

Typeset in Espresso.

Printed by Tien Wah Press, Malaysia.

10 9 8 7 6 5 4 3   789/0

AN AUSSIE NIGHT BEFORE CHRISTMAS

Adapted by Yvonne Morrison
Illustrated by Kilmeny Niland

A Scholastic Press Book · Scholastic Australia

'Twas the night before Christmas;
there wasn't a sound.
Not a possum was stirring;
no-one was around.

We'd left on the table
some tucker and beer,
Hoping that Santa Claus
soon would be here;

We children were snuggled up safe in our beds,
While dreams of pavlova danced 'round in our heads;

And Mum in her nightie, and Dad in his shorts,
Had just settled down to watch TV Sports,

When outside the house
a mad ruckus arose;
Loud squeaking and banging
woke us from our doze.
We ran to the screen door,
peeked cautiously out,
Snuck onto the deck,
then let out a shout.

Guess what had woken us up
from our snooze,
But a rusty old ute
pulled by eight mighty 'roos.
The cheerful man driving
was giggling with glee,
And we both knew at once
who this plump bloke must be.

Now, I'm telling the truth—it's all dinki-di,
Those eight kangaroos fairly soared through the sky.

Santa leaned out the window to pull at the reins,
And encouraged the 'roos, by calling their names.

GO THE ROOS!

WOOLLY JUMPERS ARE COOL!

MY BIG FAT BEAUT UTE!

'Now, Kylie! Now, Kirsty!
Now, Shazza and Shane!
On, Kipper! On, Skipper!
On, Bazza and Wayne!
Park up on that water tank,
Grab a quick drink,
I'll scoot down the gum tree.
Be back in a wink!'

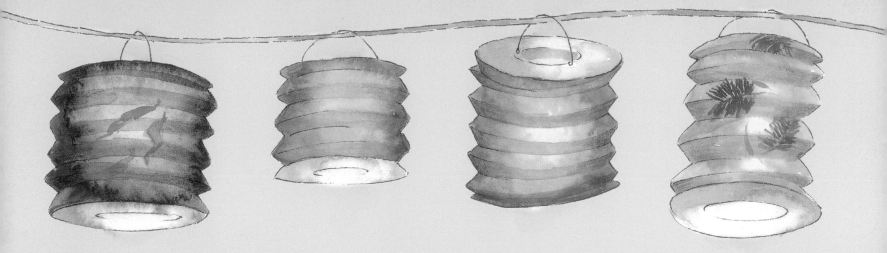

So up to the tank
those eight kangaroos flew,
With the ute full of toys,
and Santa Claus too.
He slid down the gum tree
and jumped to the ground,
Then in through the window
he sprang with a bound.

He had bright sunburned cheeks
and a milky white beard.
A jolly old joker
was how he appeared.
He wore red stubby shorts
and old thongs on his feet,
And a hat of deep crimson
as shade from the heat.

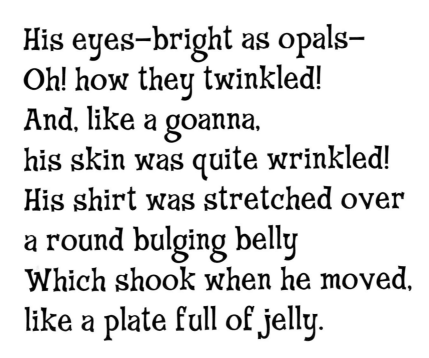

His eyes—bright as opals—
Oh! how they twinkled!
And, like a goanna,
his skin was quite wrinkled!
His shirt was stretched over
a round bulging belly
Which shook when he moved,
like a plate full of jelly.

A fat sack of prezzies
he flung from his back,
And he looked like a swaggie
unfastening his pack.
He spoke not a word,
but bent down on one knee,
To position our goodies
beneath the Yule tree.

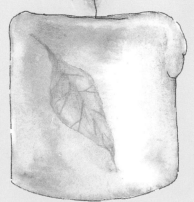

Surfboard and footy-ball shapes
for us two.
And for Dad, tongs to use
on the new barbeque.
A mysterious package
he left for our mum,
Then he turned and he winked
and he held up his thumb;

He strolled out on deck and his 'roos came on cue;
Flung his sack in the back and prepared to shoot through.
He bellowed out loud as they swooped past the gates—

'Merry Christmas to all, and goodonya, mates!'